i *might* still be in love with her...

*the PD ALT version

*written
by
blythe
stone

this
book
is
for
all
the
sweet
girls
who
might
day
dream
about
their
hot
exes

holiday
parties

CHAPTER ONE

The holidays are happening and for once I am at a loss for what to do. Usually I'm more than excited to go crash with a friend. See their new house, drink their champagne, allow them to whine to me about how hard it is to decorate for such a big holiday. This year? That doesn't sound as much fun. Maybe I've done it too many times? Or maybe it's just been way too long since I've been back home for a nostalgic family holiday.

All I know is, the week before vacation, I got this sinking feeling in my gut. A feeling that meant: *okay, Olivia it's finally time to go home.*

My family is loving enough. There is nothing exactly wrong with them or chasing me away. I've just been trying to be seen as independent for so long that I forgot I don't really have to be. I can afford to get sentimental now. It's not like there are sentiment police.

The feeling struck. I booked a hotel room and I didn't

think twice about it. At first, I only thought about my family. How happy they would be if I surprised them.

Then I thought about all the little things I missed about being home during Christmas time. My mom's tendency to want to make every single type of cookie known to man. The way my dad would always hide in his workshop playing old Christmas crooner records, heatedly talking politics with his brother, and smoking his Christmas pipe. The way our big tree looked in front of the front windows.

I thought about not being alone. Not feeling alone.

Friends are great but home is still home.

Beyond my family, there aren't many people out this way who I want to see. Okay, but the thought of seeing one person in particular really does spark a flame.

There's this girl in town. And she was my high school sweetheart. That's such an odd thing to even think about or say. I didn't know she would be coming home. From what I've seen, neither of us tend to stick close to home. But she *is* here. I saw it on her Instagram. And now I'm all fluttery and nervous. And it's almost like no time has passed since we were in high school.

She is the first girl I ever had sex with.

The first girl I ever even kissed.

A person I used to care about more than the existence of the sun.

I always wonder too, what if I never had her? Would I even know that I'm gay if she hadn't been the one to awaken all my cravings like she did?

We mostly lost contact after high school. It was a quiet falling out. All my friends say that's super normal but I don't know, it's always rubbed me the wrong way. Not because I feel jilted or hurt. But because we were honestly so good together. Like every second of our time, I felt happy. It still hurts now to remember that we're not even friends.

So, yeah, I do think about her.

I do wonder what might happen if we accidentally crossed paths.

CHAPTER TWO

I'm at my hotel now. Winding down from a pre-Christmas feast with my family. I am also trying not to think about the pretty girl in town who I often dream about but never talk to.

To stop my mind from spiraling, I posted a picture I took earlier at a coffee shop I used to go to all the time. Then I posted a selfie of me from the family party: semi-drunk and most definitely feeling myself.

I scrolled to try to find another picture. I'm so bad at remembering to post that I usually get distracted and never do.

A ding sound comes from my phone and I look at the new notification.

Avery: *Hey there, I see you're nearby. I'm in town too! Any way we can meet up for a little?*

She sent the message over Instagram. A private message. My heart went into a full blown panic. I did not know what to say back.

I know how Instagram works. She can see that I am most likely staring at the message. Not answering! Just staring! Which *is* a problem.

Avery: *No pressure of course. I just love to see you.*

I swallow hard. She is always so good at flirting with me. How sweet is that?

What a sweet way to put it. She didn't say: I *want* to see you. She said: I *love* to see you.

As in: *I follow your Instagram. I saw you post a selfie in this town. Your face, specifically? I do still love that particular face.*

I smiled and bit the side of my bottom lip.

Olivia: *Of course! I'd love to see you...*

Ug. Okay...

Comparatively, I really suck at this. Ellipses generally equate to stress. And yes, it is true. The thought of seeing her right now does stress me out. Not because I don't miss and adore her. But because life is a big complicated mess and I don't know if my brain remembers us correctly. I don't actually know if I should mess our past up by saying yes to a late night invitation to see her again.

Avery: *Where are you?* *I'm laughing, by the way, you*

*make my cheeks hurt** **You're always so shy.**

Olivia: I'm staying at the Inn on the Hill

It's a nice hotel we both know. It's also predictable that the knowledge of my worries would induce her to feel more calm.

*Avery: Of course you are *winky face**

Okay. This is… Progress? I don't know… Something *like* progress? Maybe.

Avery: Are you busy tonight? Can I stop by?

Truth be told, I just got back from entertaining the family. Something that Avery is all-too familiar with herself. A daunting task involving long drawn out stories and lots and lots of food. My parents are always telling me I need to eat more.

Avery: If you were visiting your family I can bet you're not hungry.

Olivia: A drink?

Avery: Yes please!

Olivia: Give me a little time at least?

Avery: Oh, you know I want to.

I laugh to myself. Avery used to wait for me for hours while I took forever getting ready for things. She used to lay on my bed or sit on my couch. I'd be in and out of every room like some chaos agent: trying things on, moving stuff around, hunting for earrings. Every time I walked by she'd be openly staring at me, trying to get me to stop or to kiss her.

I honestly don't know what to say to her now. How did we go from being what we were back then to being this, this - *almost* - nothing?

It's perfectly crushing. The main ongoing tragedy of my life.

But, at least, for the holidays, she did message me.

CHAPTER THREE

It took me a while to get ready but I hurried nonetheless. I'm the shorter one and the bookish one but I've more than come into my own. I've found a confidence in my silence that others have yet to embrace.

We decided to meet each other in the lobby bar. There are no expectations, AT ALL. But, while we were apart, I did dream about seeing her often. The dreams were almost always sexual. We almost always ended up kissing an naked in bed.

I've always been aware that she probably doesn't think about me. Not because I'm not interesting or anything like that but because life is busy and short and people meet and break up all of the time.

Most people don't fondly think back on a ten year old love affair that only lasted a little over a year.

And, I will confess, I never thought of our meeting

again happening like *this...*

I don't know why but this never came up in all my far-flung fantasies. Coming home is inevitable but meeting her alone in this specific expensive hotel? On the eve of Christmas? Where I have a private room and a private bed?

Something about that feels extra special to me.

In reality, I always thought we'd run into each other somewhere random and unromantic like a grocery store or a gas station, buying butter or something mundane and typical like that. We never were in the same city but in my fantasies I still had all these lust-filled dreams. It's like she followed me and accompanied me all this time, only she didn't even know it.

I pulled my black dress up over my skin and tried to imagine that I could achieve being normal tonight.

Ever since Avery private messaged me my heart has been pounding like a kick drum.

I picked up my clutch and nervously took the elevator down.

As I stepped out in my heels, I knew that I was shaky from being so nervous and so out of place.

"Olivia?"

The voice was a dream; so sweet, so familiar. A rare elixir that healed several of my open wounds.

All our memories. It was like not a day had gone by since we had been standing in the same room like this and she had been speaking my name.

"Avery," I near-gasped with relief. The years had been nothing but kind to her. She looked fantastic, all toned and sun-kissed in her tight little dress with her beachy blond hair.

I stepped forward and pulled her into a hug. Her arms slipped familiarly around my body, deliciously holding me in close and tight against her form.

"You look…"

She didn't speak the rest of her thought. My eyes closed tight together as she tenderly squeezed me.

"Good, I hope," I whispered near her ear.

"Yeah," she huffed a sexy laugh. "Yeah… You always look good."

She let me go and I shakily found my thin heels holding my weight up again. I looked down at my hands.

"Um - we should - um-" I couldn't stand the way she openly stared at me, it made me SO nervous. I pushed my brown hair back behind my ear and motioned toward the hotel bar.

"Right! Yeah," she laughed. "Let's have a drink," she said, pressing her hand to the small of my back and keeping a careful distance but not so careful that she didn't reveal that she remembered just how we used to touch. Just how we used to be.

CHAPTER FOUR

The lobby was decked out for Christmas. There was a gigantic tree filled-up with lights and bulbs, a large gold star at the very top. From the bar, we could both see it. It rained in; all these pretty colors, onto the polished and wood grain floor. There was a doubt in the air that this was indeed Christmas Eve. Wreaths and paper-wrapped presents took up all the spaces that were usually empty.

We decided on a high-top table, close to the dance floor since the bar was a little cramped. I put my clutch down and tried not to act nervous.

The woman across from me was a virtual stranger but boy did I remember her. Every little thing.

"Ooo, I like this," Avery said. She reached out for my hand and ran her thumb over one of the silver rings I was wearing. This one was vintage and it had an opal in the center.

"Oh! Yeah, thanks. My mom," I shrugged.

"She was always so good at picking out jewelry."

"She was," I laughed. So Avery did remember. She remembered a lot of things.

"So um. What-"

I laughed uncomfortably. Which made her laugh.

She had caught me staring at her. Like a deer in the headlights.

In the middle of staring I made myself speak but I didn't have a purpose at all. I just knew I shouldn't be staring as I was.

I wonder if she knew how much I loved her still.

"What?" She posed, trying to help me along with my question. Unlike me, she was not afraid to openly stare.

"Are you visiting your family?" I tried.

"Yes," she smiled and nodded. "Yes. I am afraid, I am visiting my family."

We both laughed.

I licked my lips and tried to ignore all my cravings. I wanted to touch her, to kiss her. My hand kept trying to get closer to hers.

Avery *very often* had a girlfriend. The actual girl

might switch out every now and then but she never appeared single on her socials. I didn't know what was happening in her life right now. So it's not like I could lean in and kiss her and have that be okay.

And that was truly unfortunate because otherwise I actually might.

"My dad wanted to do the trip out to the mountain like we used to. I missed the last two trips."

"Oh wow, I remember that.. Yeah," I breathed. My heart was pounding so fast. The alcohol and the nerves were really getting to me.

I knew she rarely came home for Christmas. If she did come home it was only for a short visit. In the past, if I did come home, I wouldn't know Avery had been in town until I had already left.

A big part of me kind of thought she wanted it that way. But now there was this? If she actually wanted to avoid me she certainly wouldn't have hit me up.

"Are you okay?" Avery wondered.

It hadn't occurred to me that she might be worried about me until she asked.

"Ummmm?" My voice raised.

"No," she laughed and I laughed as well. "No. Of course you're not okay."

"Are you?" I wondered.

It's better to distract myself when I feel like this. Any focus on me can make it much worse.

"No," she smirked and shrugged. "But I am *really* happy," she said, gazing at my eyes and my face.

Really happy? I thought. *Like the kind of really happy someone might be when they are in a committed relationship and seeing someone?*

"It's scary," I confessed, thinking about it.

"What? Seeing me?"

"Yeah," I laughed, feeling nervous.

"Oh," she squeaked, guilty now. "I- I don't want to hurt you."

"No-no," I rushed to erase that thought from her mind. "It's just- we haven't seen each other."

"Yeah," she breathed.

I realized then that her hand was still on the table. After she had touched my fingers she kept her own so close to mine that it made my entire body buzz, alive with pure wanting.

"I um- I liked when we did that, you know?"

"Hm? Did what now?"

"Oh!" I laughed, "sorry. I was still thinking about what you said. About why you're here. Cutting the tree with your dad."

"Right!" Avery remembered. "Yeah. God, you were so cute when we did that."

"As opposed to now," I laughed and took a sip of my martini.

"Hey! No! Stop! You're definitely cute now as well."

I swallowed the hard liquor and wondered why she even wanted to come out here and see me.

I was not a delight. But she was sure reacting to me like I might be. The way she stared was all adoration and love.

"You were so quiet," she remembered. "Scared to hold my hand."

"You told me all these stories about your dad," I reminded her. "About him being tough on you in the past and hard to read. Meeting him was a big deal."

"Yes," she nodded and remembered. "But. I don't know, it was just cute to see you like that. All soft and nervous with your green beanie and leather boots. And once you did hold my hand, you held it *so* tight. I never forgot what that felt like. I think about that trip every year."

I put my glass down on the table and stared down at the transparent base since I really didn't know what to say.

The way we were talking. The way my heart rushed.

It was like nothing ever changed. Like we picked up right where we left off.

Absolutely nothing had changed.

She remembered my clothes? How shy I had been? The way I held her hand?

It was only the one Christmas that we had.

She remembered my clothes...

"Jesus Christ, I want to fuck you." Her voice got that sexy low humming quality that it always took on when she was confessing her secrets to me.

"Hm?" I looked up and noticed her expression then. She must've been staring at me the whole time I was lost in my mind.

My mouth twitched into a smile but then my smile waned because what if that's all that this was?

One fantastic Christmas booty call...

"Sorry," she breathed, embarrassed by herself. "I knew I wanted to see you but- actually being close like this is a lot."

I wasn't insulted in the least. My heart was pounding hard. But, somehow, her confession bought me an ounce of calm. I felt more comfortable before her.

"Does this mean you're single?" I teased.

Some people missed sex a lot when they weren't

with someone. I never had that problem myself. Sure, I'd have insufferable sex dreams that made me wish I was with someone in particular but I never needed to actually go and use someone else to feel better about that.

People are different though. Avery could be different.

"It does," she laughed. "But yeah, I- don't- think that's why," she said, staring at me.

So... what is it then?

I'm not about to ask her.

This is too precarious now.

"I like that you told me," I teased her.

"What- uh- I mean- good!" She laughed, recovering. "I was going to ask you the same thing though."

"If I'm seeing anyone?"

"Yeah," she nodded nervously. "Are you?"

"I am, sort of free- for the moment," I lighty shrugged.

"Hm..." Avery thought about that.

"What?" I wondered. She always did this thing where she thought about me while she openly watched me. It was clear that she was deep in her mind. But there was also this wonderful intimacy that I didn't much feel with anyone else.

"That's just interesting," she said, taking a sip of her holiday drink.

"Can I try?" I asked, leaning in and pointing to the sugar and cinnamon that coasted the rim. It was an old fashion glass and I knew there must be whiskey inside.

"Please," she said, pushing the drink into my hands.

I pressed the rim to my bottom lip and tilted the glass until the cool spiced liquid swam its way over my tongue.

Avery watched me and I watched her back. Drinking together had definitely become an excuse to exist in the same space without much else going on.

"That's good," I laughed. Her drink was much better than mine. Stronger too.

"Do you want one?" Avery wondered affectionately.

"I do," I smirked. I knew by now I was flushed. My chest and my cheeks. There was no way in hell I could manage to hide this level of attraction from anyone. Though Avery might see it as me not having enough food in my system to handle the alcoholic strength.

Avery got up and walked until she was by my side. "Wait here," she whispered.

A lightning strike of wanting shot down through my skin. It jolted my heart, slithered down past my stomach, contracted my sex, and eventually zapped it's way down to my toes.

I held it all in, pretending it wasn't a full-body assault on my system for her to be close.

The perfume she was wearing mixed well with the whiskey and cinnamon. As her long blonde hair drifted past me I could smell the pine from the tree that she and her father had probably manhandled after chopping it down.

Avery had always been a classic California girl. Too much time on the sand and in the trees. Too much sun. An over-abundance of happiness.

I remembered all of our nights together in what felt like the one split second it took for her to travel off to the bar to grab me a drink. When she came back, I was definitely not ready to continue our patient conversation. I wanted to get her alone and allow her to rip my clothes off. Like she already expressed she wanted to do.

I stood up next to my chair and picked up my drink.

"Uh-oh," she worried. "I hope I didn't offend you before."

I smiled and shook my head. "It's not that," I confirmed.

"Okay," she said, nervous now since I was standing beside the table instead of sitting down in my chair. I took a drink and then another before setting my glass back down.

There was just something I wanted to do.

I walked closer to her and slipped my fingers down her arm until they carefully caught touch with her hand. "It's Christmas," I whispered to her.

My hands took hold of hers and I pulled her up to stand and walk with me over to the dance floor in front of the stage.

The music had been so sweet this whole time. It was romantic and it affected me. I kept on thinking: *we should be dancing.*

"You wanna dance," she realized. But I had already gotten my arms up on her shoulders. Her hands had landed on my waist. By the time she realized what I wanted we were already doing the dancing thing.

"Yes," I laughed, emotional. "Yes, I want to dance."

But that wasn't the whole of it. I didn't just want to dance. It wasn't just that it was Christmas. Avery was here and I wanted to dance with Avery. It was her.

"Okay," she softly said.

Our bodies were so close then and all it took was the

mere suggestion.

A live band was staffed, playing slow Christmas-themed jazz for lonely travelers such as myself.

We moved our way closer to the sound.

I slipped my forehead in the crook of her neck and felt her arms tightening around me like they used to when we were most certainly in love.

It was intimate. Sexy. And just like that, we were quietly together again.

Avery didn't talk and neither did I. I stroked her body in places with my hands. My breathing intensified.

Every touch seemed to be kindling to my quick growing flame.

Avery did the same, breathing my hair, feeling my curves, seeing what it was like again to be with me.

One song stopped and then another began. Every minute was an excuse now to hold on to one another like we used to before the world got hard.

The band played on. We were caught up like this for several songs. I held the back of her neck and breathed in a way I had nearly forgotten I used to.

"Alright folks, we're going to take a little break," the singer smiled.

We both let go of each other and clapped with the other dancers who had been cozy out on the dance floor.

It was hard now. I knew what I wanted and I knew that at least she still wanted to sleep with me.

I looked over at our table and saw that it had been taken. "Oh shoot," I said, nervously.

"It's okay," Avery smiled and tugged me in closer to her. I loved her hands on my body, the way I really did feel like I belonged to her somehow. "Let's get you another drink."

"What about you?" I asked.

"Me too," she laughed. "We'll get me one too."

We sat at the bar this time on the tall chairs. I couldn't help but notice that she had not stopped smiling this entire time. I scooted in closer to her and let her hand fall down onto my inner thigh so I could hold it there.

"So, tell me about where you've been," she tried.

"Oh!" I laughed, too flushed to even think. We had just sinned on that floor. My body was alive like we had done purely sexual things. It was like we were back in high school again. Just the thought of touching produced sparks. "Yeah, I don't have any answers about that."

"Don't do that," she laughed at me and flirted. "Do you have any idea what it's like sitting cities away from you and seeing you appear up on my screen?

It's like torture," she smiled.

"Yeah, you look really tortured," I teased her back.

"No. Fuck. I mean it," she beamed, frustrated. "What even happened with us?"

"You left," I shrugged.

"Hey," she said, hurt. "We both left," she reminded me.

"Yeah, but I didn't really think we were breaking up," I confessed.

Avery tilted her head to the side and looked sad. I slipped my fingers between hers and held her hand. Then I rubbed her arm with my free hand. I didn't want her to feel sad.

"So what's it like for you then?" Avery wondered.

"What do you mean?" I laughed. "What's what like?"

The truth was, I had been waiting back then. We both went off to different colleges and I was waiting, for a little while. For her to call. For her to say she missed me and it was a mistake. But then I saw that she was seeing someone. It all happened pretty fast.

"You never talk to me," she swallowed emotionally. I watched her lean forward and suck a little bit of the cool liquid from her little red straw.

It was sexy, being near her. Everything about her was overwhelmingly sexy. Her smell, her hands. The way her body looked in her dress.

"You started seeing someone," I shrugged.

We were young. Stupid. And hey, maybe she was right, maybe I should've talked. I did try but I've never been a very obvious person.

"Baby..." Avery sadly sighed.

"It was a long time ago," I reminded.

"Yeah, but still..." She said, "I thought we both agreed it would be too hard to stay together."

"We did," I remembered. "Verbally. We did."

"But you waited?"

"Yup," I said, pathetically.

I never wanted to break up with her. She wanted to break up and I let her go.

Avery was staring at me now like I was the most perfect human she had ever seen. It was enough to make me want to push her off her stool just to get the staring to stop. It made me feel all these intense things. Stuff I remembered from a long time ago when she used to be mine and she couldn't keep her hands off of me.

"Okay, you need to stop looking at me like that," I laughed.

"Okay," she nodded and turned to look at her drink.

"Do you think it's pathetic?"

"No!" She yelled over the talking and the cheering from the other bar patrons, some of whom were having an after-work party in their ties and white shirts. They'd suddenly gotten much louder and the band had come back. "It's sexy," Avery yelled.

And I smiled so intensely that I felt happiness swirling around inside of my stomach. "Well, thank you!" I yelled back.

"What?! Why are you thanking me?! I'm apparently a big asshole!"

"You're not," I stared over at her and shook my head.

A big part of me back then just thought there wasn't enough of me to want to keep. Which made all of this really dangerous and messy but I missed her so much I was willing to throw myself at a storm.

Avery watched me while she took a big sip from her drink. I couldn't take it, so I slipped forward off of my chair and stood up again, pulling a few bills from my clutch and placing them up on the bar.

"Uh-oh, what's happening now," Avery wondered. I had slipped my body close into hers. It was hard to even breathe when we were this close but this was the only way out.

"Come up with me," I whispered near her ear.

I knew that she would. She already expressed exactly what she wanted from me tonight. This wasn't about catching up or feeling lonely. Avery saw me online and she realized she wanted to have sex with me again.

I started to move and she got up to follow me. Our fingers touched and she held mine.

It was late now, much busier. Turns out a lot of people schedule parties and reunions inside of hotel bars and lobbies during Christmas time.

I pulled Avery inside of the elevator and pressed the button three times fast to try to get the door to close us in all on our own.

"Hey, you know we don't have to do-"

I turned and pushed her body back. Her back hit against the wall of the elevator.

No more waiting or thinking. No more hoping.

Avery was here, we were both having a good time. I was taking advantage of that. I pushed her back and took my shot. A split second passed and I was suddenly kissing her just like I used to when we were both young.

It was like a dam letting go inside of me. As soon as my lips parted, our tongues touched. I was back there in that before time where things made much more sense and all my feelings were free flowing liquid and lust.

I kissed her deep, not thinking about it or holding myself back.

At one point, I gasped inside her mouth, unable to restrict myself.

The elevator dinged and I moaned reflexively.

"Fuck," Avery bit.

"Come on," I said, leading her down the hall and to my room.

Avery was sweet and quiet. Her hands pet me adoringly. She wasn't one to take advantage. Always worried that she might break me or cause me pain. And she did once. She did break me and cause me pain, but she didn't know it. She thought it was mutual, until now.

When we got in the room it was my turn to be taken. Avery turned me in the dark, her hand found my face and she led her tongue inside my mouth again.

It was fast and perfect. My body was being pushed down onto the clean bed. Avery's body was sliding up onto mine, reminding me of what it used to feel like with just her and me. The hours we'd spend on top of each other, kissing like this and touching all night.

"Did it always taste like this or am I just fucked up right now," she whispered needily.

I felt her kissing down my neck and electrifying me.

My hand swam up to my head. It was so much all at once, and honestly so unexpected, that I couldn't even answer her.

She slid down my body, not even giving me a chance to respond or breathe.

Before I could talk she'd tugged my underwear down, slipped her tongue inside my sex and tasted me.

In the silence of the room, I gasped and tensed my body. One of my hands slipped into her hair and onto her head while the other clasped at the white down comforter on the bed, squeezing the fabric as if it could somehow steady me.

"Yes," I heard her breathe.

The next noise out of me was an animal cry of pure and undiluted pleasure.

I came against her, fast and wet, and she crawled up my body and sucked on my breast.

I cried out again and this time she slipped her fingers inside of me.

"I missed you," she whispered, all sexy and dreamy against my neck.

Until now, I couldn't think. But I paused to wonder if this was only about the sex.

She's inside me and I'm feeling things. I've already cum once so I can be calm enough to wonder where this is going and if she wants me in the way I have always hoped to have her.

The odds of us being on the same page are slim to none.

I let her bring me to another climax. I suck on her perfect fingers while I cum.

How is it even possible that she's not taken?

I crawl on top of her. My hair cascades down around us as I find her mouth again.

The rest is a wonderful, wonderful dream...

CHAPTER FIVE

The kissing lasted long into the early hours of the morning. I'm pretty sure that part is my fault.

When we finally stop, I kiss her chest and curl my body against hers. She lets out a breath with her hand on her head. "Okay, I didn't think it was possible that you could get any better."

"Stop," I laugh.

"It would be nice if I was but I'm not joking," she said.

"Okay," I breathed, unsure of what I should say.

"Are you okay?" Avery wondered.

I shrugged and laid my cheek down on her skin. Words weren't my favorite any more. I lost her due to words and now I was wary of them.

She rubbed my back and kissed my hair. "I hate that we haven't talked."

"I'm sorry," I whispered.

"It's not your fault," she said.

"It's hard for me," I reminded her. Avery is such an honest and upfront person. I hide my feelings because I'm scared of letting them free.

"I know," she whispered sweetly. "I just meant... all these years," she explained. "Not tonight. I love tonight... I love everything about tonight."

It was so sweet and I knew I might cry.

I kissed her chest again and found my energy to kiss down her body but she stopped me.

I bit my bottom lip and stared into her.

"It's better here," she said, brushing her lips with her fingertips.

I smirked and crawled back up her body. And here I thought I was being too sappy, forcing kisses onto her.

I kissed her hard and felt my body alight from all the friction. "You're just being nice to me," I breathed.

"I promise you, I'm not," she said, rubbing my ass with her hand as she kissed me again and bit my lip.

"Fuck," I pinched out.

"Is it okay to admit I'm a little mad at you right now?" Avery asked.

It scared me and stressed me out. I let my forehead fall down onto her body. "Oh no," I breathed.

"No," she laughed, "come back, come back."

She led my chin back up so she could sweetly kiss me.

"You taste really good," she whispered to me.

"Why are you mad," I wondered. I was definitely love-drunk now. Also, emotional. I propped my head up on my hand and swallowed nervously.

"I wish you had talked to me," she said.

"When?" I wondered.

"All the time," she laughed and touched my face.

I smiled sadly and stared down at her lips. "I knew what you wanted," I reminded.

It wasn't my place to seek her out. She'd set me out on a raft on the ocean.

"Yeah but *I* didn't," she laughed, implying that maybe she'd made some bad mistakes.

"That's okay," I said and I kissed the back of her hand.

Her eyes gazed at me so I shut my own and moved her thumb over the tip of my tongue so I could suck on it.

"Fuck," she pinched out.

The bed of her thumb was soft inside my mouth and I felt her in my sex as I sucked on her. It was strange how some people didn't even have to touch your sex for you to feel them there. Life was always like that for me with Avery.

Her breathing quickened and I knew I was turning her on, causing her chest to heave.

"We could've had a completely different life," she realized.

I moved back onto her and started to kiss at her neck. "We're not dead," I teased.

I could feel her heart beating a mile a minute as she let out a laugh.

"Touch me," I asked. And her hands found me then, stoking me and holding me. I licked at her neck and she held me close.

I fucked her again, knowing that she ached more for me now and that it would feel that much better for her. I wanted nothing more than to hear her aching voice inside my ear.

CHAPTER SIX

Light shone in through the large windows and I woke to the feeling of warmth on my face.

The clock said it was past seven. As soon as I shifted, Avery woke up and shifted as well.

"Hi," she said, catching me as I moved my body off of hers.

"Morning," I said. I was secretly happy she hadn't slipped out in the night. "I should probably shower."

"Mmm… no, don't," she smiled. "If you move I'll be all alone."

"Come with me," I laughed.

I got up and she came.

I turned the shower on and let it run. Avery spun my body and held me close to her like she had done last night when we were dancing.

"I have this unending urge to do bad things to you today," she confessed.

"The Christmas spirit?" I joked.

She growled against the skin of my neck and I laughed at her. But the longer we continued like this the more it hurt to think about the fact that we'd be parting again soon. I held her lovingly and she started to nip and suck at my skin.

"I want to fuck you," she whispered achingly.

"Fuck me," I breathed, more ready for it than she could ever even know.

She took me under the water and pressed my back up against the tiled shower wall. It was tender and loving. So good that I wept. I didn't want it to ever end.

After the shower we were sweet and quiet with one another. I put my underwear on and put on some jeans and a soft emerald cropped sweater.

Avery put her dress back on. I watched her and felt sad.

"Do you have to go?" She wondered.

"A bit later," I said.

I didn't want her to feel like she had to stay.

"What about you?" I asked.

"Dinner," she nodded. "I could go," she shrugged.

I walked back to her and touched her face. She wrapped her arms around my waist so our bodies would be touching.

"How did I fuck this up so bad," she moped.

I rested my head on her shoulder and gave her a hug.

"Can I take you to breakfast?"

"I'd like that," I whispered.

"Good because I don't want to leave you..."

CHAPTER SEVEN

I was wrong to think the lobby was busy last night. Now it was bustling with people and families. I'd never stayed in an expensive hotel like this around Christmas time. As we passed the commotion Avery squeezed my hand and pulled me in closer to her so that she could hold her arm around my lower back.

"Merry Christmas," she smiled.

"Yeah," I laughed. There were decorations everywhere. A real-live santa was standing around telling a story to someone over his smartphone.

"I got you something," Avery said.

"What?" I said, surprised. She didn't even know that she'd be seeing me? How could she get me something?

"How?"

"I have my ways."

It was chilly out but not too bad. The sun surely helped. When we got to her car Avery made me wait outside.

"Okay," she said nervously. "I have a confession."

She handed me a big wrapped box. It was pretty with old fashion style brown wrapping paper, some green ribbon and soft twine. I took the box and nervously watched her.

"Okay, I do this thing," she laughed at herself. "Where I think of you all the time and don't really tell you about it."

I swallowed and tried to reconcile that.

"You *could* tell me," I reminded.

"Yeah but, I don't know, it never seemed right, so..."

I fingered the twine and wondered how often these thoughts of me really occurred. Were they only when she was single? Only this week? This year?

"So, you don't have to open it now but- when you do- know that those gifts are from different places at different times in my life over the years."

"Avery..."

She groaned and looked embarrassed. "Yeah- yeah. I know," she said. "I just suck at getting things to you apparently."

I stared at her openly as I pulled on the twine and made it come loose.

Her eyes were so beautiful in the daylight. It was addicting to stare at them. Somehow I knew that I had forgotten how entrancing they were.

Avery helped me to open the package and inside was just as she said, several different little things. A couple of rings. A stuffed bear with a bow. Some earrings. A pair of soft socks. Many things. The most surprising were the cards from several years ago. They each had notes inside which made me cry.

All these years... She wrote to me *all these years* and I didn't know.

"I'm sorry," she said. "I know it's probably angering. I wasn't sure if I should give those to you."

"It's good," I said, emotional. "I didn't know that you thought about me."

"Aaaaand that- makes me want to kill myself," she sadly laughed.

"Please don't," I asked and reached for her. I put the box down on the seat and stood back up to give her a hug.

"Did you know that I would be here?" I wondered.

"No," she confessed.

I hugged her even tighter and kissed the side of her head.

"I'm not sure I can get you anything to compare with that," I confessed.

"You already have," Avery comforted. "I've wanted to see you for so long. Talk to you. Find out if you're okay..."

I leaned back and stared up at her. Her gaze shifted down to my lips.

There wasn't a piece of me that thought I should resist any part of this. I pushed up on my toes and gave her a kiss. As I did, her arms tightened around my body and squeezed. We didn't need to ask if it was okay. We both wanted to make-out in the middle of the parking lot like we were two kids.

My head spun and I already wanted her inside me again.

"At least let me buy you a coffee," I eventually said.

"Okay," she rolled her eyes and laughed at me. "Okay..."

I kissed her again, not wanting this to end.

Avery let me go and I reluctantly got into her car.

CHAPTER EIGHT

Breakfast was nice. We didn't manage to talk about much. Too busy staring at each other.

A couple of Avery's old friends recognized her and came over to us. I could tell she was a little bummed and nervous to be talking to them. It interrupted whatever was happening with us.

It was okay though. I personally didn't mind it.

I sipped my coffee and occupied my mind with the memory of last night and our morning in the shower.

In the parking lot, we flirted and dawdled. All the way back to the hotel I was sad.

Avery parked the car and a tear streamed out of my eye.

"Oh no!" She worried, turning to me.

"It's okay," I laughed.

"No it's not," she smoothed my tears with her thumbs and laughed.

I kissed her sadly and tried to push all my depressing thoughts away.

Avery kissed me again and again. Each time much deeper than before. I tugged my boots off and pushed her back in her seat, crawling on top of her.

It was a mad sort of lust. A desperate need to never stop touching.

Her hands slipped beneath my sweater as we kissed, rubbing my back, holding my sides, squeezing my breasts. Eventually we stopped and she just held me for a little bit.

"I don't want you to go," she said.

"If I don't, they'll worry."

"Okay," she spoke sadly. "Are you staying another night?"

I paused then. It hadn't actually occurred to me that she might want to see me again.

"You don't have to answer, if it's too much," she quickly said.

"I am," I breathed.

"Can I come back later? See you again?"

She pushed my hair away from my face so that she

could look at me.

I nodded and stared at her in each of her eyes.

"Okay," she breathed. I could tell that it pleased her to know that this wasn't the end.

She pulled me in and kissed me emotionally.

We couldn't kiss for long. But we stretched it out until the very last millisecond.

CHAPTER NINE

My parents always had the most expensive looking decorations. They were the type of people to hire out a service to do it up right.

They invited my entire family. It was a huge gathering and I quickly became lost in the fray: friends, neighbors, aunts, uncles, step cousins.

I drank several alcoholic beverages and ate more food than I'd ever fully remember.

At the end of the night I called a car to take me back to the hotel.

In the parking lot, I saw that Avery's car was already there. I smiled and walked over to it. When I put my hand on her window she lowered it down.

"How long have you been here?"

Avery smiled and shrugged.

"I would've left you a key."

"You look sleepy," she smiled.

"Yeah," I laughed.

When she got out of the car she was wearing jeans and a thin black top. I could see her collarbone and my hand wandered up to touch the necklace that she had put one that I bought her a long time ago.

I fingered the pendant and stared up at her.

"You should've let me take you to that party," she said.

"You wanted to go?"

"I wanted to be with you," she corrected me.

I smiled softly and watched her with affection.

"Can I buy you a drink?"

I nodded.

We walked together, hand-in-hand, back into the hotel.

CHAPTER TEN

I told Avery a few new stories about my parents. She knew them and remembered my life.

We were sleepy but we kept on talking for a long long time.

"I'm supposed to go back tonight," she randomly said.

My face dropped then and it was probably visible but I tried to correct it.

"I have work tomorrow. Well I was supposed to have work."

"You're not going?" I asked.

Avery looked at me and shook her head.

"How long are you staying," she wondered.

It was Christmas night and all I wanted for Christmas was her.

"I haven't decided," I lied. I was supposed to go back tomorrow but I could cancel my flight.

"Okay," she sighed. "But how long *were* you staying?"

"Tonight," I confessed.

"Hmmm," she hummed and tried to read me.

It made me nervous that she knew me so well. I felt hot in my sweater and I knew I was flushed.

Avery reached for my hand and lightly held it. "Let's go up to the room," she said, putting off any talk of this ending.

"Okay," I said. I didn't want to have to think about it either.

CHAPTER ELEVEN

We rode the elevator up. The whole time she held me close with my back against her front.

When we got back up to the room I took my heels and my sweater off. I hadn't worn a tank top.

"It was really hot down there. I think I have to shower again."

"How about a bath?" Avery wondered. She surprised me, sneaking up behind me and pulling my back into her body.

"Okay," I breathed. I was trying to avoid touching, since I felt a little sweaty.

"You still smell really good," she whispered in my ear.

I smirked and huffed a small laugh. "I'm all sweaty," I

spoke nervously.

Avery's hand stroked my neck as she breathed me in near my ear. Her other arm was firm across my stomach. It was sexy and I wasn't sure what I should do.

"It's hard to be out with you in public and not think about doing this..."

I breathed loudly, already turned on. She turned my body and kissed me passionately. Somehow I ended up with my back to the wall. Her hand swiftly undid my fly and my zipper. Before I knew what was happening her tongue was inside me and her eyes were gazing up at me from below.

"Uhh!" I let out an uncontrolled cry.

Her hands tugged my jeans further down my thighs and her tongue drug itself over my clit with so much precision and pressure that I knew I was going to explode.

It was fast and then her fingers were in me again. Her body pushed in against mine, holding me steady. I stared into her eyes as she perfectly fucked me inside.

No more thoughts about taking a shower. I pushed her back onto the bed, stripped her clothes off and teased her with my body for a long time before really helping her out.

It wasn't fair that she was so damn good at making love.

How was I supposed to think about anything else when she could do that?

CHAPTER TWELVE

Hours later we were both pleased and tired but still refusing to settle down. There had been some screaming and a fair amount of begging too.

But now we were back to our soft petting, our seemingly endless kiss-a-thon. She was sitting back against the headboard and I was straddling her lap.

"Do you think this can work now?"

"I don't see why it couldn't," I said.

We lived in different cities. Had very different lives. But we didn't have to live in different cities. And we didn't have to have very different lives.

"How do you feel about Los Angeles?"

"Not opposed or against."

Avery worked in Hollywood. She had always worked in a place that needed her to be in a certain place at a certain time so I knew it was a big deal, even right now, that she was blowing off work.

"Or, I could come to San Francisco..." she posed.

I suddenly needed to know why she was ready now when she hadn't been ready for several years.

She was playing with my breasts and sucking on them. I was sitting on her lap, straddling her thighs and trying to keep my shit together (which was very hard).

"Why now?" I breathed, overcome by even the thought.

"I honestly didn't think you would ever want to talk to me again," Avery confessed.

"Does it look like I don't want to talk to you?" I teased.

She stared up at me and my mouth fell open as she sucked on my nipple again.

I heard her laugh against me. Then she hugged my waist tight so my sex would rub against her body. It rocked me inside. I hadn't had good sex in years and she was always so great at it.

"I was mistaken," she apologized.

"And what of these other women you've seen?"

She hugged me tight again and sucked on my nipple hard before kissing it.

"None of them were you," she said.

And I honestly wouldn't know if she was making it up or just flirting with me.

"I think we should try," I said. I was at a point in my life where I missed her more than I craved anyone.

"Mmmmm," Avery smiled. She shifted her body, holding me carefully as she led me to lay down onto my back. "That makes me happy," she said.

She kissed up my skin and held my hand back against the mattress, above my head.

"Unless you plan on hurting me," I added on.

"Yeah, I wouldn't," Avery said. Then she kissed my neck and found my lips again. "I wouldn't hurt you," she said. And when she kissed me this time she plunged her tongue so deep inside. I felt my sex release and clench. Her hand held my neck and her thumb stroked my throat possessively.

I wrapped my legs around her waist and knew for sure that I was a goner.

We couldn't stop touching and we obviously remembered each other fondly from back then.

"I wish I'd been stronger," I breathed.

Avery held my hands and pushed them down against the bed. Then she thrust her sex in against mine. "You're strong," she breathed, hovering sexily over me.

"Do that again," I asked. And she squeezed my hands and rubbed her sex against mine again.

I didn't want to be talking anymore. I wanted her hands on my skin, her body quickly moving.

"You're so sexy," she breathed.

"I'm not," I huffed a laugh.

"No, you are," she confirmed. All the while, she never stopped rubbing against me.

CHAPTER THIRTEEN

The day after Christmas I woke late to find myself alone in my hotel bed.

The clock said it was after ten thirty. I instantly worried that I slept way too long and missed saying goodbye to Avery.

If she left, she left.

I crawled out of bed and snuck into the shower to clean myself off.

There could be several reasons that Avery had to go. One of which could've been that she's scared. I get that. We were strangers, then hot and heavy. Maybe that's scary for her. I couldn't know.

When I got out of the shower I jumped to find Avery sitting on the closed toilet seat and waiting for me. She had a holiday coffee cup in her hand and she looked shockingly beautiful like she'd gotten up early and spent a long time getting ready for me.

"Sorry," she laughed. "I didn't mean to scare you. I just went to get us some coffee."

I pulled a towel onto my body and started to wrap myself up. "It's okay," my voice shook.

My heart had picked up. There was a hurt inside. For a few minutes there, I actually thought she had left me. That she wasn't coming back.

Avery put her coffee cup down. Then she stood and tugged on me to get me to turn and give her a hug. "What's wrong? Are you okay?"

"Um... No," I said. Her arms had already enfolded me.

"What is it?" She wondered. She was being so careful and loving with me.

"I-" My voice caught inside my throat as if I was choking.

"Shhhhh," Avery soothed me and held me against her. "It's okay."

"I- *thought-* you left," I let out.

It surprised me. That I could let those words go. That I could say them outloud. It was like, all this time I had been holding on and I didn't even know.

"I wouldn't," she comforted.

"Okay," I said, trying to calm myself down.

Avery held my face and she started to kiss my neck. I tilted my head and that's when I felt her everywhere.

"It could be possible I should never have let you go," I breathed.

Avery took my towel out of my hands and pushed it off of me and onto the ground. I felt her hands grope my body. Then she slipped her fingers down the backs of my thighs and lifted me up against the wall.

"Maybe we can fix it," she sweetly said. Her body leaned in against mine and held me up.

"Stay with me until the new year," I posed.

"Okay," she sexily breathed.

"That was way too easy," I laughed at her.

"I think that's good. Don't you?"

"Mmhmm," I breathed, far too taken to want to talk anymore.

She overtook me then, kissing me hard and touching me like I was her everything. I swam in her wake, floating on top of it all, in pure ecstasy.

There wasn't going to be a time when I'd regret this. I knew that much.

For now, I let her take me and play with me. This year she was, for sure, my Christmas present.

AUTHOR'S NOTE

It was REALLY hard to decide on where to end this one. I kept on stopping and then adding - stopping and adding. I must've ended it at least three times before finally stopping it where I did.

Just thought I should put something out since it's been so long!

If you're interested in more of this adventure, let me know! I might be persuaded to write a new year's continuation!

Happy Holidays!

and, as always, if you're looking for something longer to read - check out the Paper Dolls book series